PRETZEL
AND THE
PUPPIES

PAWS UP!

Margret and H. A. Rey

Clarion Books
An Imprint of HarperCollins Publishers

Welcome to Muttgomery, city of dogs!

It is home to the Doxie family: Pretzel, the World's Longest Dachshund, Greta, the mayor of Muttgomery, and their five frisky puppies.

Family time is the Doxies' favorite time. Pretzel and the puppies love to play the game I Spy as they walk Greta to her job at city hall.

This morning Pretzel asks,
"Who wants to go first?
Paxton? Pedro? Pippa?
Puck? Poppy?"

Poppy wheels up and says, "I spy with my little eye someone we see almost every day."

Her brother Paxton wonders if it could be Mr. Kibble at the market.

But it is Pippa who correctly guesses, "It must be our mail dog, Ms. Pupperpost!"

"Good morning!" the puppies call out.
Ms. Pupperpost is like most dogs in
Muttgomery—doggone friendly.

She replies, "Hello, Doxies!
I've gotta zip, but
have a great day!"

It's Pippa's turn to choose an object and she says, "I spy something that's sooooo colorful!"

"Is it this hydrant?" asks Puck.

"What about these chew toys?" guesses Poppy.

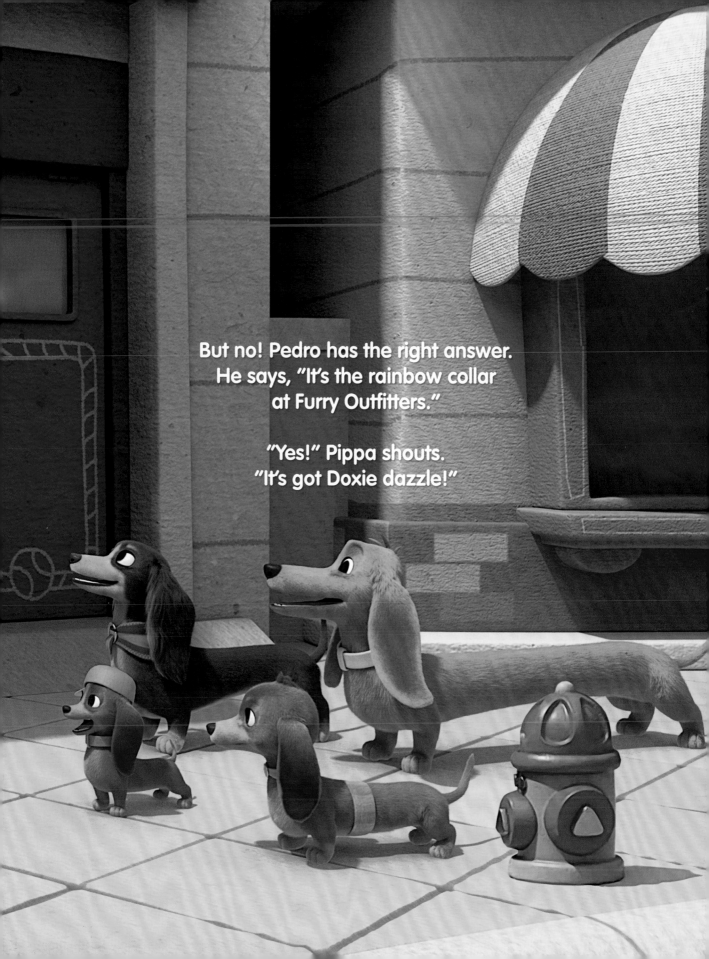

But no! Pedro has the right answer.
He says, "It's the rainbow collar
at Furry Outfitters."

"Yes!" Pippa shouts.
"It's got Doxie dazzle!"

Paxton looks around. There are so many wonderful things to see in Muttgomery! The pups could play I Spy all day.

But then he notices something not-so-wonderful in Puppington Park.

"I spy something really big and blah. Something not colorful," he says, sniffing.

Two neighborhood dogs walk by.
One of them suggests that they sit on a bench in
front of a bare wall. But the other dog quickly says,
"Let's move somewhere nicer."

"Oh, I get it," Puck says to Paxton. "You spy that big, empty wall. No one wants to sit near it!"

Greta agrees, "This wall is definitely not
as colorful as the rest of Muttgomery."

"I spy Paxton getting an idea!" Pretzel says.

Paxton's tail wags with excitement. He pants,
"We should paint a picture on the wall!
Something big and bright. Then everyone will want to
have picnics and play fetch in this part of the park."

The family thinks this is a bark-tastic idea!
But where do they begin?

"Well first, you need to talk
to the mayor," Greta says.

Paxton grins. "But Mom,
you are the mayor!"

She smiles at her pup and says, "And I think it's a great idea.
We'll need the town council to vote on your proposal."

"Come on, let's go see them now!"
the puppies yelp.

The family arrives at city hall. The town council dogs are welcoming. Their names are Mr. Shaggs, Ms. Clawtez, and Mr. Bernard.

"Good morning!" Paxton says right away. "Did you know there is a big, boring wall in the park? I'd like to paint a mural on it— something as colorful as the rest of Muttgomery!"

Mr. Shaggs says, "I've never liked looking at that wall!"

Ms. Clawtez suggests that the council votes on Paxton's plan. Happily, they all raise their paws to vote yes.

Mr. Bernard says, "It's unanimous!"

Unanimous means that all of the council voted the same way. Paxton can paint his mural.

Bow-wow!

"Come on," he yips. "Let's go home and get my painting supplies!"

At their house, Paxton says, "Let's paint pictures on our easels and then pick one to paint on the wall!"

The pups use brushes and paint to fill up their empty canvases.

Some pictures have bright colors.
Some have bold shapes.

"You all had great ideas! Now we can
pick one," Paxton says. "But there are
so many. I can't decide!"

Paxton doesn't want to let anyone down.
"Hey, Paxton," Pretzel said.
"Don't get yourself tied up in knots.
Get those paws up! You can do it!"

Paxton shakes his ears and stands up straighter.
"Okay, paws up! Come on pups," he tells his brothers and sisters.
"If we're going to figure out which picture to paint,
we should vote like the town council!"

Paxton puts a piece of paper in front of each picture.
He says, "Make a paw print under the picture
you want to vote for."

When the pups finish voting,
each picture has a lot of votes.
There are more paws than they can count.
And so many wonderful colors.

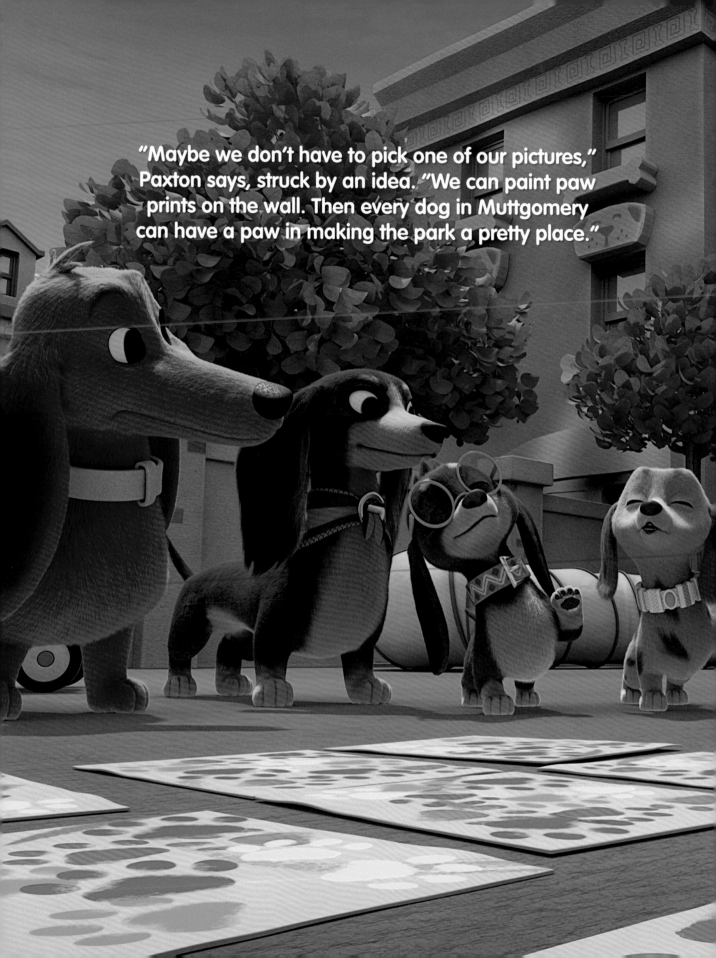

"Maybe we don't have to pick one of our pictures," Paxton says, struck by an idea. "We can paint paw prints on the wall. Then every dog in Muttgomery can have a paw in making the park a pretty place."

Every pup votes

YES

to that idea!

When the Doxie family arrives at the wall with
their painting supplies, curious dogs gather around.
Paxton speaks up:

"Hi, everyone. Let's make this wall just as
colorful as the rest of Muttgomery. All you
need are your paws. . . and this paint!"

The dogs of the town put their
paws up and get to work—
teamwork!

They begin to make their
unique marks on the wall.

When they finish, the wall is no longer blah, it is *beautiful!*
Look at all those dogs spending time together in the park.
Have you ever seen so many wagging tails?

"You sure made your bark today, Paxton," Pretzel says.

"Made my bark?" Paxton asks.

"That means, you made Muttgomery a better place for every dog that lives here!" Greta says.

Even small dogs can make a big difference.

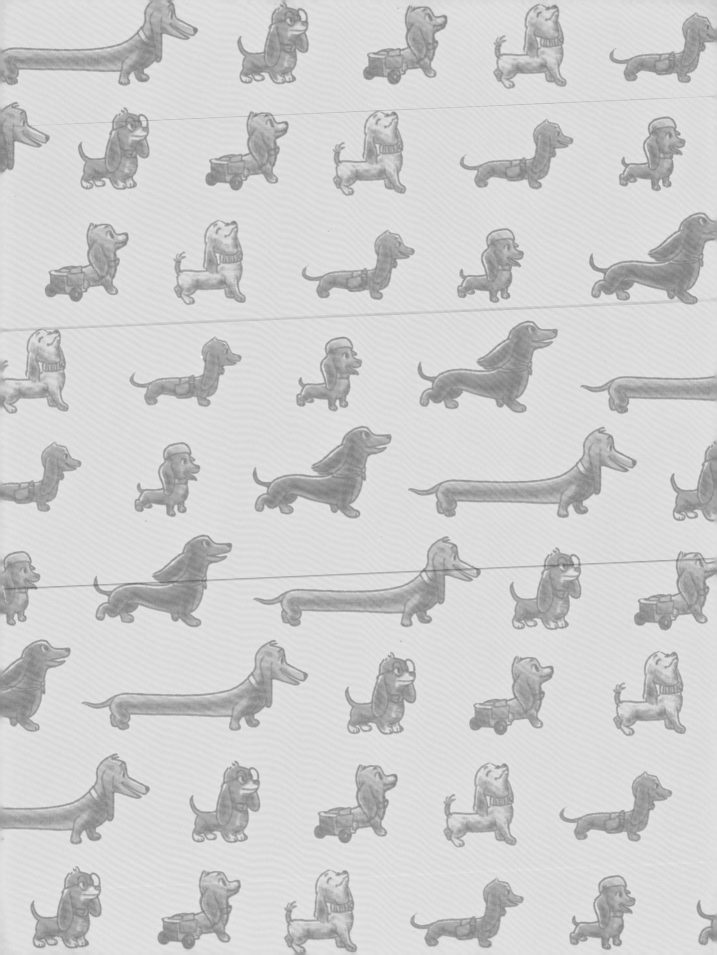